May you always seek and find the TRUTH!
Barbara Seregi

The Truth About Hazel's Cookie

STORY BY BARBARA SEREGI

ARTWORK BY KIMBERLEY GAMEZ

Oliver and his younger sister, Hazel, were playing with their toys when their mom walked in and asked them, in her perky voice, "Guess who's coming over later today?"

"Who?" they asked, together, excitedly.

"Tag!" their mom said.

"Yay!" exclaimed Oliver, smiling while Hazel clapped her hands.

They loved Tag. She was the most fun and funky babysitter, always in bright and colorful outfits. She also, usually, let them play whatever they wanted, as long as nothing and no one got hurt.

Later that day, the doorbell rang. Oliver and Hazel jumped up and ran to the door.

"Yay, Tag is here!" shouted Hazel.

She arrived with a big smile on her face, carrying a large, blue purse and wearing blue pants, a golden yellow shirt, and a white belt with a large "T" belt buckle.

Mr. and Mrs. W exchanged hellos with Tag as Oliver tugged on his mom's skirt and said, "Bye, Mom, bye, Dad!" excitedly.

The children's parents laughed, kissed each child on the forehead, and said goodbye.

Tag called out, "Goodbye, Mr. and Mrs. W. Have fun on your date!"

She closed the door and walked to the kitchen.

"Time to eat dinner, you two," Tag sang.

She gathered food from the refrigerator and prepared it.

Oliver and Hazel sat down at the kitchen table as they all chatted, excited to see each other.

Meanwhile, Chloe, their cat, strolled by, rubbed her side on Oliver's chair, then walked through the living room and disappeared down the hallway.

After they had all
finished eating
hamburgers,
strawberries and
carrots, Oliver
asked,
"May we have the
cookies that Mom
made now?"

Tag smiled and said, "You have finished all your dinner, so, yes, you may have one cookie each!"

Tag gave each child a cookie and went to clean up the dishes and the counter.

Oliver peeked into the living room and said, "Look, Hazel, there goes Chloe."

Hazel turned to look for Chloe but did not see her. She was confused.

Then she looked at her plate, and there was no cookie there!

"Hey, where's my cookie?" Hazel asked.

Oliver asked, sheepishly, "Huh?"

Tag turned from
doing the dishes
and saw Hazel's
cookie gone, and
Oliver's half-eaten
one in his hand.

Tag came and sat down at the table, looking first at Hazel.

"Hmm," she said. "What could've happened to Hazel's cookie, I wonder?"

Hazel cried,
"Oliver took it!"

"No, I didn't!" Oliver shouted. "See, I don't have it!"

He held out his hands to show that they were empty, as he put the last bite of his cookie in his mouth.

Hazel did not believe him. "Yes, he does! He took it! Give it back, Oliver!"

Tag looked at Oliver and said calmly, "Surely, Oliver didn't take it. He's an honest boy. He knows it is not right to take things that don't belong to him. He wouldn't do that."

Oliver and Hazel stared at Tag.

Tag only said, "Hmmm."

Everyone was quiet for a couple of minutes and sat there, thinking.

After a while, Oliver turned to his sister and said, "I'm sorry, Hazel."

He took the cookie out of his pocket and handed it to her.

"I just like them sooooo much."

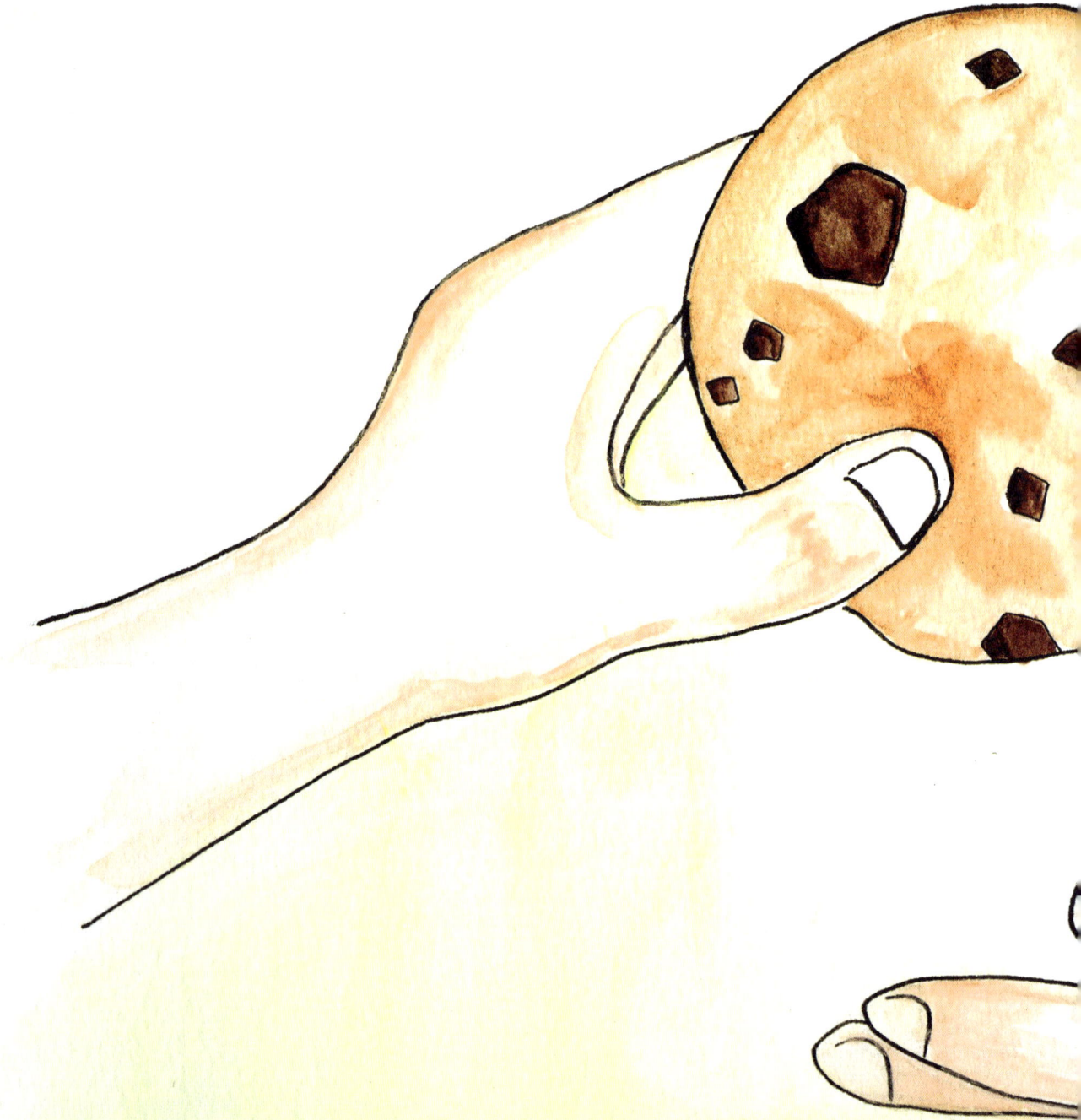

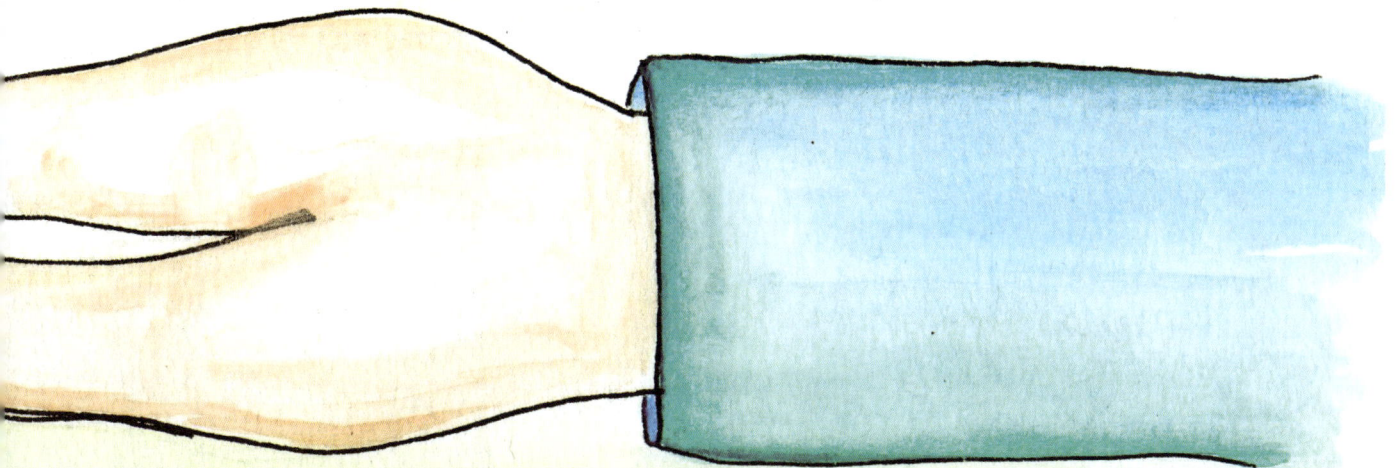

Hazel replied, "I know. I do, too! I accept your apology."

Tag smiled and said, "Don't you feel better that you told the truth?"

Oliver nodded. "Oh, yes. My stomach hurt before, and I couldn't even eat the cookie."

Tag explained: "That's your conscience making your stomach feel that way."

Oliver looked puzzled. He asked, "What's a conscience?"

"Well," said Tag, "It's your mind knowing right from wrong. Your mind knew it was wrong to take the cookie, so your stomach hurt from not telling the truth."

Tag continued: "You see the T on my belt? It stands for two things: Tag, my name, but also, Truth. Truth is the first part of the armor that God gives us to protect ourselves. If we tell the truth, God will help us and our conscience will be happy. And you know what that means?"

Oliver exclaimed, "YES, my tummy is also happy!"

They all laughed.

Hazel then finished her cookie, took Tag's hand, looked at Oliver, and said, "Come on, guys. Let's go play!"